For Daniel Goldin

First published 1997 by Walker Books Ltd
87 Vauxhall Walk, London SE11 5HJ

10 9 8 7 6 5 4 3 2 1

This book has been typeset in
Stempel Schneidler Medium.

Printed in Italy

British Library Cataloguing in Publication Data
A catalogue record for this book is available
from the British Library.

ISBN 0-7445-4972-8

WILLY THE DREAMER

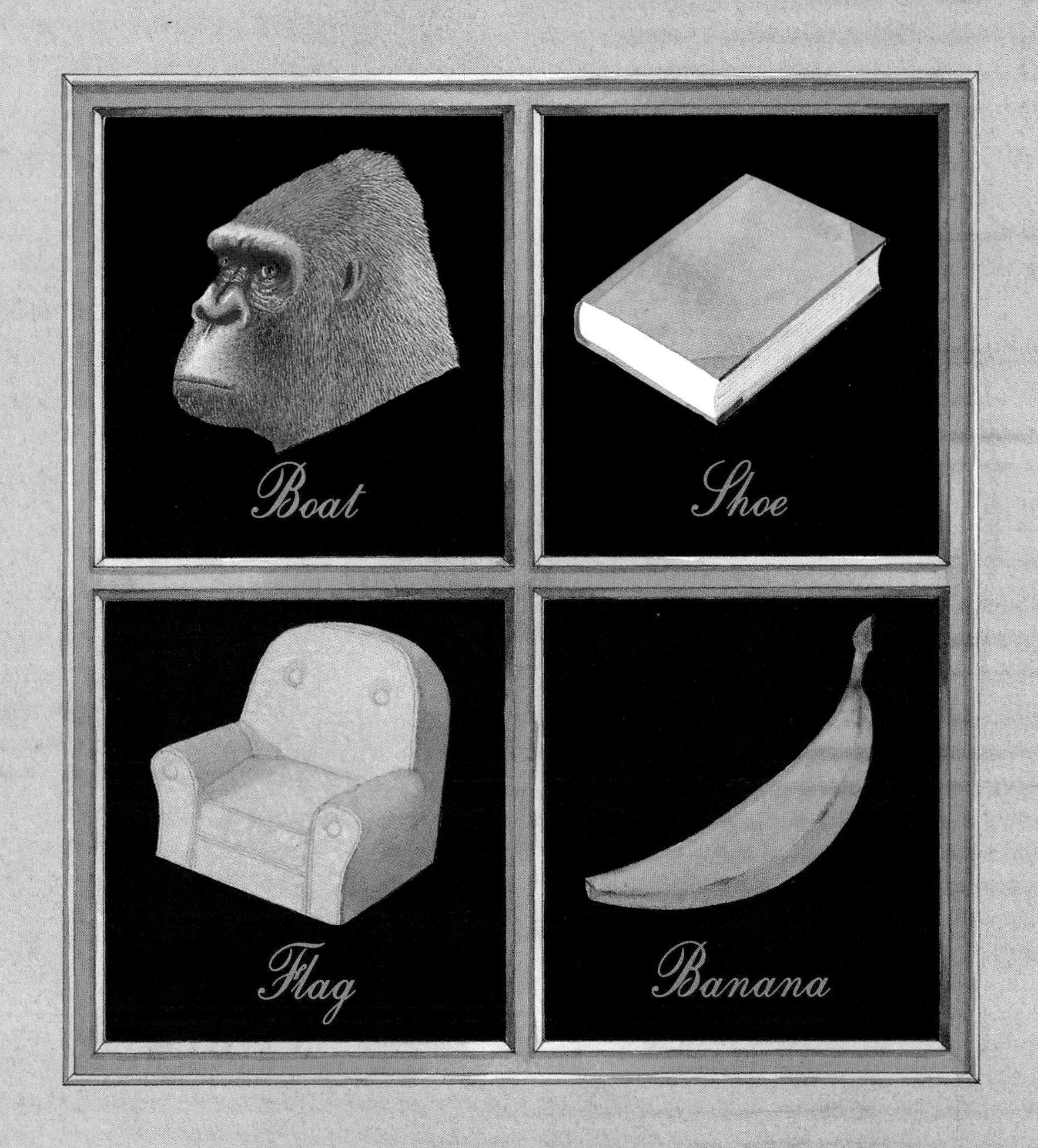

Anthony Browne

Willy dreams.

Sometimes Willy dreams that he's a film-star,

or a singer,

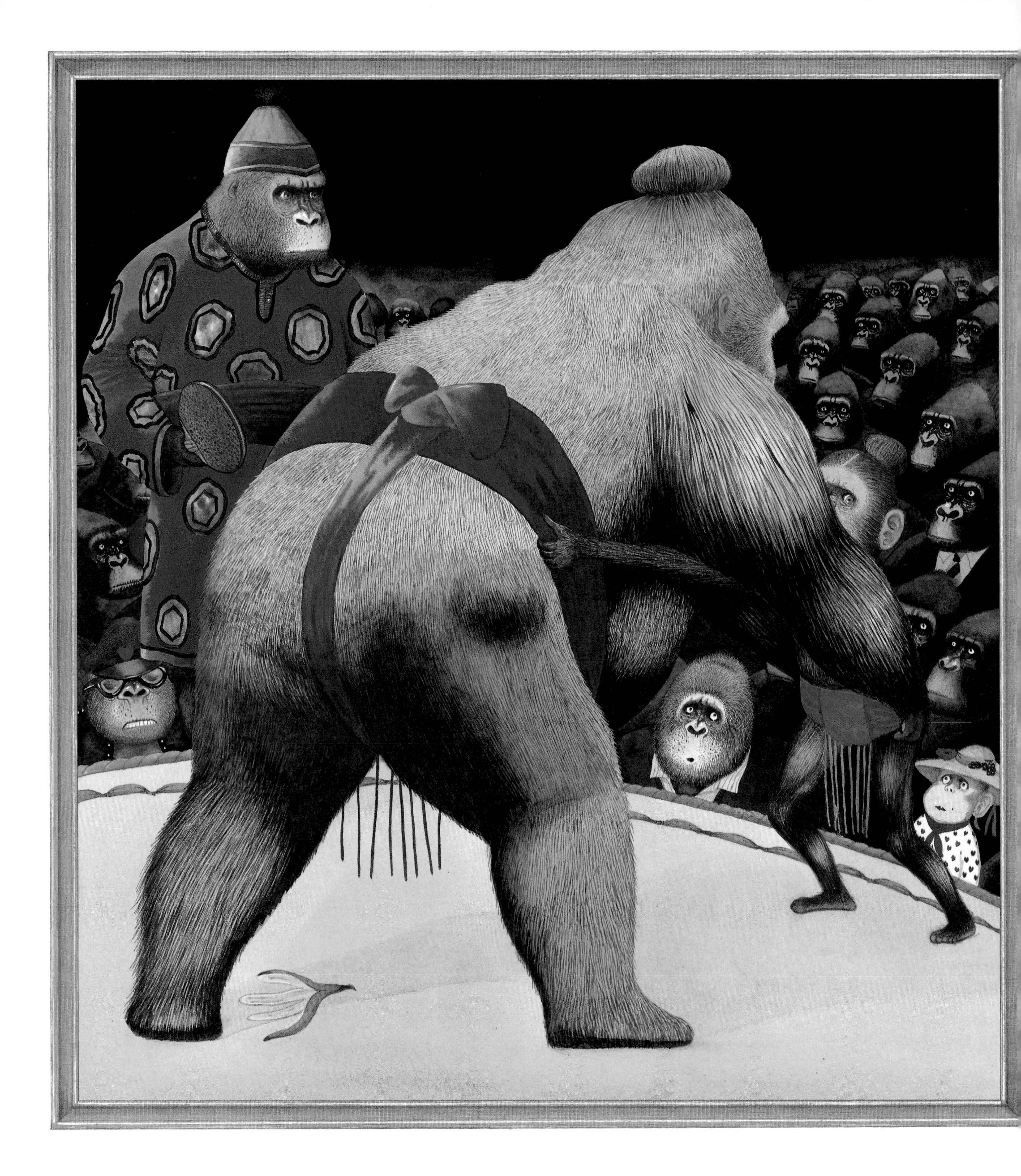

a sumo wrestler,

or a ballet dancer… Willy dreams.

Sometimes Willy dreams that he's a painter,

or an explorer,

a famous writer,

or a scuba-diver... Willy dreams.

Sometimes Willy dreams that he can't run

but he can fly.

He's a giant,

or he's tiny… Willy dreams.

Sometimes Willy dreams that he's a beggar,

or a king.

He's in a strange landscape,

or all at sea... Willy dreams.

Sometimes Willy dreams of fierce monsters,

or super-heroes.

He dreams of the past ...

and, sometimes, the future.

Willy dreams.

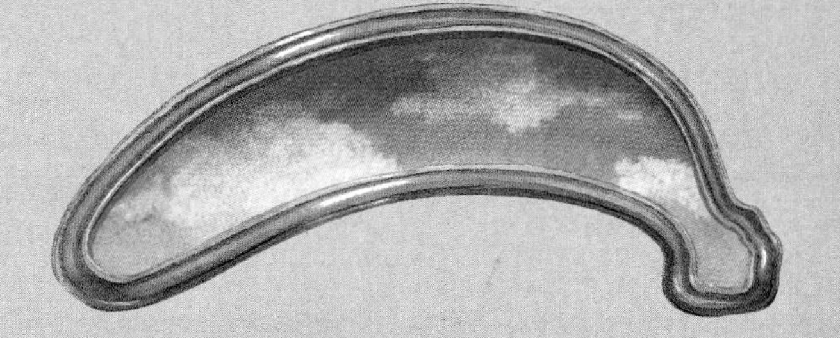